HOW TO DATE
AND MARRY
THE RIGHT
BLACK WOMAN

A White Man's Perspective

Which Black Women to Pursue,
Which Ones to Avoid,
Which One to Marry!

By Jeff Brandon

Legal Disclaimer

For those who can see beyond the surface..

Table of Contents

__Introduction__

Women come in all shapes, sizes, and racial backgrounds. I've dated many different types over the years—Asian, Black, White, Hispanic—all were unique and exciting in their own way. As a white man, ironically, many of my most enjoyable dating experiences were the times I spent dating black women. There was something different about it—for some reason it was more fun and intriguing to me. Once acknowledging my dating preference, I focused my attention solely on interracial dating, and have spent a majority of the last 10 years dating mainly black women.

With the help of online dating, I was given the opportunity to date black women from different parts of America, and from different parts of the world. These experiences introduced me to unique personalities, ideas, and cultures—it gave me the chance to explore dating habits and behaviors of black women from many different walks of life. These experiences quickly showed me the positive things that a relationship with the right type of black woman could bring. The experiences also showed me the turmoil that dating the wrong type of black woman could bring. Unfortunately, I dated many of the wrong ones before I got the opportunity to date some of the right ones. The right ones seemed to be somewhat harder to find, especially in America, where racial division and fatherless homes rule the day. Like anything in life, when you're new at something, you need patience, it can take a few tries to get it right. Nonetheless, it was these real-life dating experiences—the good and bad—that gave me the motivation to write this book.

If you're a white man thinking of dating black women for the first time, you shouldn't jump into it without getting valuable insight on the subject first. This book will give you that insight, plus important tips on how to gracefully navigate your way through the wrong ones and get you on the fastest track to the right one—for a successful interracial relationship.

Most of the instruction and advice I give in this book can be applied to women of any race or culture. However, with interracial dating, especially when it comes to a white man dating a black woman—you'll be confronted with discrimination and certain roadblocks you normally wouldn't have to face. This book will guide you through those roadblocks and quickly get you on the right track to the type of black woman you should be dating.

Interracial dating should be filled with lots of fun and excitement. To make that happen, you first need to be dating the right woman. This book will instruct you on the type of black woman you should be searching for—and where you should be looking to find her. I'll also teach you how to avoid costly mistakes that could hinder your chances of interracial dating success. After reading this book, you'll know which black women to pursue, which ones to avoid, and which one to marry.

This book can also be very beneficial to black women who are new to interracial dating, and new to dating white men. Getting an inside perspective on white men's dating habits and preferences can be of great value—especially when it comes to seeking a successful interracial relationship.

Chapter 1
Interracial Dating With A Black Woman Is Unique

Most people with any dating experience quickly realize, in order to have a strong relationship, you must have more things in common than just physical attraction. With black women, it's no exception. You must have similar interests, shared core values, and most importantly, a natural ability to communicate. Communication becomes even more crucial when it comes to a white man dating a black woman. You may face challenges from family, friends, and even some everyday people in society. You'll have to be focused—and be on the same page with each other mentally to achieve success.

A white man dating a black woman can potentially attract a lot of attention—sometimes unwanted attention, even stares. But don't mistakenly assume the attention and stares are all negative. Most people simply like viewing something they don't get a chance to see every day.

While most people will be pleasantly intrigued with your interracial love interest—on rare occasions you'll provoke the opposite reaction. You and your date might be the target of an ugly comment from someone in a crowd you walk through. You and your date might get a mean glare from a passing person on the street. These types of incidents are rare—just always be aware of the possibility and be prepared to respond appropriately to the situation, just in case something escalates. Just like the philosophy taught in martial arts—it's always best to simply walk away from silly insults and pettiness from people—especially if the situation doesn't place your love interest in any kind of danger. In all my interracial dating experiences, I can only recall two negative incidents. They were mainly negative comments, and they were both from black men who seemed to dislike the idea of a white man dating a black woman.

When dating interracially, you can't expect everyone to approve of your dating preference. Doing so will only leave you disappointed and frustrated. Some people won't be thrilled with the idea of you dating a black woman no matter what you do, and that's okay—don't take it personally.

Get comfortable with the idea of being only one of a few—if not the only—white man at social gatherings. Sounds funny, but some white men have rarely found themselves in a social setting where they're the only white man in the crowd. When dating a black woman, you could potentially find yourself in that situation. When this occurs—and it's likely to happen eventually—try to be friendly and approachable. It will be worth your trouble. She will notice and appreciate your effort. Being in somewhat awkward social situations you've never been in before is one of the bigger adjustments to interracial dating with a black woman. Just like anything else though—the more you do it—the better you'll be at doing it.

Remember to always be yourself and don't try to force things. As white men dating black women, sometimes we try too hard to win people over. We think because of the negative stereotypes out there against white men—we need to prove to her friends or family, we're "good guys." Don't do it. It'll only come off needy and fake, and that's not the way to make her more attracted to you. Black women, like all women, are attracted to confidence. Trying way too hard doesn't display confidence.

Most would agree—one of the most enjoyable and exciting parts of dating is the time spent getting to know each other. With interracial dating, it's even more exciting. Exploring the differences between you and your date can be endless fun. Take the time to learn about each other's culture and upbringing—look at the differences and similarities. It will give you a lot to talk about and will present a great opportunity to develop a deeper bond with each other while doing so. That's exactly what you want, especially if you can see yourself with her in a potential long-term relationship!

Chapter 2
The First Date

That first meeting with the black woman you're trying to impress can be a very exciting moment. Of course, you want to make a great first impression, but you don't want to come on too strong. No matter how friendly she appears, it could be her first time going out with a white man and she may need time to get comfortable with things. If it's your first interracial date, try not to let it show. If you look uncomfortable—she will pick up on it and she will begin to feel uncomfortable. Be calm and relaxed. Like any first date, the more natural you are, the better the date will go. It will help her begin to relax and enjoy herself.

Remember, it's a first date, you should avoid serious subjects in conversation. Try to keep things light and fun. Don't start with a dinner date, where you'll feel forced to talk. Try a fun activity like putt-putt golf or a walking tour. You can both be more laid-back, and free to roam—not stuck in a tight setting where you're sitting across from each other the entire date. One of the biggest differences between an interracial first date with a black woman compared to a first date with a white woman is the added attention from the public. This can sometimes add extra pressure—so try first date options that lighten that pressure.

As a man, you should be running things on the date—but make sure it's done in a friendly and charming kind of way. Give her some time to warm up to you. Because of the possible cultural differences between white men and black women, she might need a few moments to loosen up and get used to your personality and sense of humor.

Don't make any strong romantic moves too soon unless you get a signal from her to approach. Again, if it's her first interracial date with a white man, she may need time to get comfortable. Pay attention to her body language, you'll know when she's feeling relaxed. Once you see she's enjoying herself and reached your comfort level—then feel free to release all the romantic charm you like. She'll then be ready to open up to you, and also be more locked in on what you're saying to her. You should be working your magic from this moment on.

Chapter 3
She Likes All of Your "Whiteness"

S ome white men think they need to "act black" to attract a black woman. This is a false belief! Most of the black women I've dated in the past were very annoyed at the sight of a white man pretending to "act black." Most black women who date white men are very much attracted to a white man's "whiteness." They like most of the "white things" about a white man. Never worry about being "too white." The right black woman will like all the things that make you who you are—all the things that make you unique. A big part of that is, you are being your true, "white" self. So, don't put away your guitar or hard rock music collection, if that's what you're into—play them loudly—she wants to see the real you.

Remember, interracial dating is all about celebrating your differences. It's based on the idea that opposites really do attract. Whether people want to admit it or not—it's what keeps the relationship new and exciting. Don't try to hide or hold back your "whiteness," or waste time pretending to be something you're not. That's the opposite of what she wants from you.

Chapter 4
She Desires A Strong White Man

Most women secretly desire a strong man, whether they want to admit it or not. I've heard it said many times by black women who date white men, "I like a manly man." Trust me—mature women aren't attracted to childish little "man-boys" who wear sagging jeans hanging off their backsides. She's looking for strength from you, especially when it comes to a long-term relationship.

For political reasons, most American media outlets try to portray white men as shy, timid, or nerdy—anything but strong. So be aware of the media brain washing she might have endured. You may have to take the time to show her that the opposite is true, that white men collectively are very strong.

The media—whether it's done through TV or online—is constantly working overtime to hide white men's strength and bravado from the masses! It's not a coincidence that most American women are clueless to the fact that white men own many of the world's Olympic weightlifting records—and that specifically white men have held the title of "World's Strongest Man" since the competition began over 40 years ago. White men also hold records in professional heavyweight boxing, football, and basketball—just to name a few. It's also not a coincidence that the American media only wants people to know who the "Fastest Man in the World" is but doesn't want people to know—or even think about—who the "Strongest Man in the World" is. I honestly believe that if the strongest man in the world wasn't currently a white man, everyone in America would know who he is.

A large percentage of white men are naturally strong and masculine—it's a big part of who they are—partly because most white men were raised with strong fathers in the home to teach them how to be men. For many white men, that teaching goes back many generations. I've heard some black women say they feel "more feminine" around white men. Whatever the case may be, this natural "masculine energy" is why some black women choose to date white men.

Being a strong man goes far beyond physical strength. It's also mental strength and integrity. It's being able to make the right decisions at the right time—even when it's tough to do so. Being strong is about taking responsibility. It's being there for others when they can't be strong for themselves. It's showing humility, sacrifice, and faithfulness. These are some of the things the right black woman will be searching for in you. She wants to see it, because on the inside, she also sees some of those same qualities in herself. Remember, a strong woman secretly desires a strong man. and only a weak woman would try to date a weak man.

The right black woman will also appreciate and compliment your strength. She won't be threatened by it. She won't foolishly waste time trying to compete with you over little things. She needs you to be strong in order to consider you for a serious, long-term relationship. She needs to know she can put her faith and trust in you completely. Regardless of what you've heard, a real woman can never trust a weak man. While getting to know you, she'll be looking for your strength. Show her you have more than enough!

Chapter 5
Wait A Minute, Now She Thinks I'm A Racist Monster

As a white man, one of your biggest challenges to a successful interracial relationship with a black woman is the mainstream media. Different from local media, the mainstream media can reach a national or global audience. For political reasons, the mainstream news and entertainment industry—who both have deep political ties—constantly labels and portrays the white man as the big, bad, racist, boogeyman, solely responsible for all the evil in the world. You see it everywhere in the media, especially in news reporting. White men are constantly being stereotyped or labeled as racist bullies. If that wasn't bad enough, those same political ties have crept into other areas of popularity—many white men are now purposely being kept out of certain sports and popular music—anything that's connected to the national media. The attack is real.

The attack on white men is difficult for some black women to understand, because the attack is coming from "white men"—white men who own the media attacking the character of other white men. What they don't see is that the attack on white men is almost always driven by politics. These are "white liberal" men attacking the character of white men for their own political gain.

Most people know that America consists of two main Political parties—Democrat and Republican—more commonly known as the Left and the Right. Shockingly, strong supporters of the Left have now taken almost full control of the national media. They now own an estimated 90% of it—so they use it as a valuable weapon—mainly for their party's political agenda. In today's world it's almost impossible for someone to view a popular website, movie, or TV series, without getting some kind of political agenda or propaganda pushed on them. That's why many people now refer to the media as "fixed media" or "fake media." Even the major search engines we use every day appear to be politically slanted—search results are now thought to be mostly "fixed" and "adjusted" to push a Leftist narrative. News stories and websites that fit the Left's agenda now appear to be given precedence and rank over everything else. Even some of the comments you see on popular video sites are now thought to be "staged" just to slander and push negative stereotypes against white men—sometimes against black women who date white men.

In a general sense, the Left is the party known for giving more government handouts and assistance. They support the LGBTQ community—they tend to side with undocumented immigrants. In many ways, the Left caters to people who think of themselves as "oppressed" or "victims." Some might see this as a positive thing, but keep in mind—to keep getting votes—the Left must constantly attract more "oppressed" or "victimized" people to their party. Of course, the people they're trying to attract don't have to be truly oppressed at all—they only must think of themselves that way. The media is the Left's most valuable weapon to make people feel they're being oppressed.

Just like a car mechanic shop only needs people to think that their vehicle is damaged to get their business—the Left only needs to make people think of themselves as victims to get their votes. To produce "victims" and "black oppression," the fixed media pushes the "racist white man" narrative almost on a daily basis. The media tries to make black people think that white men are out to get them or out to hold them back. Another trick of the media is to take the racist or criminal acts of a small percentage of white men and use it to paint the majority of all white men bad. In the political world these tactics are referred to as "identity politics," or "racial politics." Also understand—there's a tremendous political gain for the Left by keeping white men and black women separated. It helps secure "oppression" votes. The Left realizes—once black women date white men, they usually fall out of the "black victim" and "white men are racist" mentality. Those black women quickly see it was mostly lies and political propaganda.

Please don't confuse the goal of this chapter. I didn't add it to pick on the Left or try to push you to the Right. I'm all for people voting for what they believe in—it's one of the greatest rights we have in America. The two parties stand for many different things that have nothing to do with race. I have friends and family on both sides of the political aisle that mean a lot to me. My goal isn't to offend. I only added this chapter to the book to help you understand the game that's being played in the media, and to help you see what's behind it. I'm trying to help you dodge a bullet. I know from first-hand experience how damaging and toxic the media can be to your interracial relationship. You need to realize, even if you don't take in much TV—even if you're not active on social media, or don't attend movies—many other people do. They indulge in these things a lot! That means many people are being influenced daily by what they see and hear in the different forms of media. That influence can affect the attitudes and opinions of friends and family close to your relationship. It can also influence the black woman you're in a relationship with. If the black woman you're dating doesn't understand the political game being played through the media, she can possibly fall victim to the propaganda, and see you as the bad guy. In the very least, she can begin to have disdain for white men in general. This won't be good for your relationship—it can only bring arguments and division. It's very important for you to discuss this topic with the black woman you're dating. The propaganda in the media can easily destroy your relationship.

Try to seek out a black woman who is unbiased and rational—a woman who is at least willing to take the time to understand important subjects she isn't particularly interested in. One of the goals of interracial dating is to seek out a fair-minded person. Anything short of that will be difficult. One advantage of dating black women outside of America—many of them haven't been indoctrinated by the race dividing media—they haven't been taught to fear or hate white men. That doesn't mean you can't find intelligent black women in America who can easily see through the propaganda—they're out there. You just need to search a little harder to find them.

When it comes to racial topics that might fall outside of politics, sometimes her perspective and viewpoint may greatly differ from yours. She may see things the total opposite of you—and that's okay—you're a white man and she's a black woman, it can easily happen. Take advantage of these moments to understand each other on a deeper level. If done maturely, these conversations can bring you much closer. It can build trust and intimacy in the relationship because you're both communicating about important and sometimes emotional things. With racial topics, the goal is to understand her view, and help her to understand yours. When you find you can't agree, strive to meet each other in the middle. The middle is a good place, it's a place that doesn't have a particular side—or a particular race.

Chapter 6
Seek Her Family's Approval, But Don't Try Too Hard

Make an honest effort to get along well with her friends and family, but don't stress over it if your efforts aren't reciprocated back to you. I learned many years ago—you can never have control over other people's opinions of you. Some of her friends and family will like you, and some won't—regardless of how well you treat them. Some may have prejudices against you, and some may simply be turned off by your personality. Taking it personally or continually trying to win them over usually ends up being a waste of your time and energy. Don't try to force the relationships.

Many women you date will share the heated arguments you have together with their mothers or sisters, even their brothers. This can keep you the bad guy with her family long after you've made up with her. A mature woman understands the damage this can cause the relationship, but she could still possibly end up doing it from time to time. Just be aware of it.

When dating a woman with children, of course things can get a bit more complicated. But ultimately the same rules apply. You can't force any of her family to like you—even her kids. Make an honest effort and try to be understanding and forgiving with them. Don't worry if things aren't perfect. If you've followed my advice so far—and you're dating the right black woman—disagreements with her friends or family won't damage the relationship you have with her.

The right black woman will always keep your arguments with her separate from your relationship with her. She will also keep arguments you have with her friends or family separate from your relationship with her.

When you're with the right woman, arguments don't stick around too long. They come and go quickly.

Chapter 7
A Black Woman's Hair Is A Big Deal

T he majority of white men who are new to dating black women have no idea about the amount of time and effort black women put into their hair. It took me years of dating black women to fully appreciate the hard work they put into it just to get the style they want to achieve. Unlike white women, black women must go through extreme measures to protect their hair and not damage it. They sometimes modify their hair with extensions and other things, which can take long hours to assemble. That's about as deep as my understanding goes on the subject—and that's probably as deep as you'll have to go as well. Having said that—her hair can be a sensitive topic for her—so there are some rules I recommend you follow to show her you appreciate and support the effort she puts into it. Try not to complain about the time she spends on her hair. Try not to touch her hair a lot unless she asks you to do so. Try to say something nice about the style she chooses, even if it's not your favorite. Try to understand, her hair is an important part of her life and the sooner you understand that—the easier things will be. Whether she admits it to you or not—her hair is a big deal.

Chapter 8
Which Black Women You Should Avoid

In today's world, an overwhelming majority of black women are raised in fatherless homes. Women who grow up in this type of environment need extra time to mature emotionally and understand their role in romantic relationships. It's the same way with men who grow up fatherless. Women who come from fatherless homes have a more difficult time communicating and relating to men. They didn't see their mothers communicating with a male figure in the home while growing up, so they lack the important reference to fall back on. Without a father—or positive male role model—women usually miss out on the opportunity for a strong male figure to show them love, affection and guidance. If the black woman you're dating didn't get those important things growing up, you might have to pay the heavy price for it. She may have a difficult time trusting you. She may have a difficult time taking advice from you or respecting you. She may have a difficult time opening up to you. These things can severely damage a relationship—no matter how strong the attraction may be. Unless she's willing to honestly work through these issues, be prepared for a relationship with this type of black woman to ultimately fail. Problems of this magnitude don't just go away; they need to be carefully worked through and dealt with—sometimes by a professional.

A black woman who won't compromise, or won't at least meet you halfway in disagreements, isn't a woman you want to enter a relationship with. This type of woman is flawed. In several of my past relationships, I dated black women who presented themselves as perfect angels, until we disagreed—they then turned into fire-breathing she-devils. These women have a false belief that if men don't fall at their feet when they're trying to get their way—they're the wrong men for them—or those men are "controlling men." These women have let the media convince them that they're supposed to "run things" in the relationship. This type of woman has a difficult time submitting to a man in any way—no matter how good that man treats her. Even if a man were to give this type of woman everything she wants— any time and every time she wants it—she still won't be happy. She will secretly resent him for being weak. Again, she is flawed. She will resent you for being strong and will resent you even more for giving in to her. It's a no-win situation! These women aren't ready for relationships. Don't waste your time and energy on them. Unless she's willing to seriously work on herself, the relationship will never work.

A black woman who can't admit she's wrong—is the wrong black woman for you. I've dated women who were so afraid of admitting to a simple mistake—they were willing to risk the entire relationship to not own up to being in the wrong. A woman with this kind of mindset can't take any responsibility and will ultimately blame you for every problem that comes up in the relationship. Thinking you're to blame for everything, this type of woman will look to end the relationship or seek out a new "knight in shining armor" to save her—not realizing her lack of responsibility is a big part of the problem in the relationship. Pursuing a relationship with this type of woman is pointless. It's destined to fail. Admitting one's faults or weaknesses takes courage and maturity. A woman who can't do it is showing you she isn't ready for a real relationship. Don't waste your time on this type of woman.

As I mentioned in a previous chapter—a black woman who puts her faith in the media, can't put her faith in you. In the past, I've been in relationships with black women who loved me one day, and despised me the next—it all depended on the latest racially charged media story they indulged in. A black woman who can't see through the fixed media will possibly resent you every time a new racially charged news story hits. You'll find yourself constantly trying to convince her that you're not like the "racist white men" she's seeing on TV and social media. If she can't acknowledge that the politically driven media pushes racial division— she will more than likely buy into the lies and eventually turn on you. You will quickly grow tired of trying to convince her that she's being deceived and manipulated. She will ultimately see you as the bad guy and the relationship will eventually fall apart.

Chapter 9
Which Black Women To Pursue And Marry

Will she respect you during heated arguments? If she treats you with respect even when she's upset or emotional—she's showing you she has a strong foundation and she won't freak out when things get tough. This is one of the ultimate signs of relationship maturity and extremely important when it comes to sustaining a long-term relationship.

Can she keep an argument separate from the relationship? If she stays focused on the argument and doesn't use the relationship as leverage to win the argument, she's a keeper. The right black woman won't use the relationship as a weapon during the argument. She won't threaten to leave the relationship just to get her way. She realizes doing that can damage the foundation of the relationship.

Can she take responsibility for her actions? Can she own up to any shortcomings she might have? If she's secure enough to admit her faults—she's showing you she's a mature woman. The right black woman takes accountability for her part in the relationship. She acknowledges that it takes two people to make sacrifices in the relationship for it to be successful.

Can she see through the media lies? If she sees through the slanted mainstream media and doesn't let the racial politics of the day get inside your relationship—she's worthy of your time and investment. The right black woman understands why the media solely focuses on racially divisive stories depicting white men as "racist" or "inherently bad." She knows the media is a political tool used to divide the country and fan the flames of racism.

Did she grow up with a father or strong male role model in the home? If the answer is yes, she'll be more open to receiving love and affection from you. She'll freely give her trust to you—you won't have to constantly convince her that you're being truthful when discussing things.

Can she laugh at herself? The black woman who can make fun of her own shortcomings is showing humility—which is a great thing—it's an important character trait to have when it comes to building and sustaining a meaningful long-term relationship.

Does she fear God? Does she have faith in God? These are both great qualities for a woman to have. The Bible tells us "Fearing God is the beginning of wisdom." If she fears God and has faith in God—she'll most likely want to live her life with a certain amount of integrity, faithfulness, and love. This is the kind of black woman you want in your corner!

<u>Closing Thoughts</u>

My past interracial relationships taught me a few important things about dating, and about myself. I found out that love doesn't have a color. It transcends space, time, and culture. When two people truly care about each other—it's their hearts that ultimately bond together—it's their hearts that keep the relationship strong—race is irrelevant.

Being in an interracial relationship with a black woman will pose some extra challenges, but those challenges fail in comparison to all the great things you'll gain from being with the woman you want to be with. Remember, nothing good in life ever comes easy.

God made all types of women—black, brown, white, and everything in between. If you're attracted to a black woman, go for it! The right black woman will be everything you need, and more—don't let a silly thing like skin tone keep you from being with the one you really want to be with.

Thank you for reading. If you enjoyed this book, please consider leaving a review. God bless.